Mary and the Fairy

by Penny Dolan

Illustrated by Deborah Allwright

D0230055

2675787

13

This edition 2009

Franklin Watts
338 Euston Road
London
NW1 3BH

Franklin Watts Australia
Level 17/207 Kent Street
Sydney
NSW 2000

A CIP catalogue record for this book is available
from the British Library.

ISBN 978 0 7496 9142 4

Series Editor: Louise John
Series Advisor: Dr Barrie Wade
Series Designer: Jason Anscomb

Printed in China

Franklin Watts is a divison of
Hachette Children's Books,
an Hachette UK company.
www.hachette.co.uk

A fairy flew in through Mary's window.

Party

"Mary, why are you so sad?" she asked.

4

"I've got nothing to wear to the party," Mary said.

The fairy smiled.

"Mary, you *shall* go the Ball!" she cried.

"Wait ..." stammered Mary.

But the fairy wasn't
listening at all.

"How about a red frock?"
asked the fairy.

The red frock made
Mary feel terribly hot.
"But ..." she said.

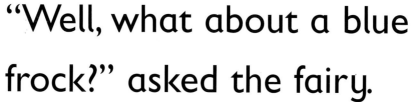

"Well, what about a blue frock?" asked the fairy.

The blue frock made
Mary feel terribly glum.
"No!" she said.

"I know! A yellow frock!"
the fairy cried.

The yellow frock made
Mary's eyes go terribly
wiggly.

"I've got it this time! A green frock!" shouted the fairy.

The green frock made Mary's tummy feel terribly wobbly. "Yuk!" she said.

"No, don't tell me ... you want a white frock!" guessed the fairy.

The white frock made
Mary feel terribly shivery.
"Stop!" shouted Mary.

"What colour frock *do* you want?" said the fairy crossly.

"I haven't got all day, you know!"

"I don't want a frock," Mary sighed.

"What I really want, is ..."

"Oh, I see!" said the fairy.

She waved her wand again.

"Is that right?" she asked.

"Oh, yes! Thank you, fairy," cried Mary.

"Now, I shall go to the fancy dress party."

Puzzle 1

Put these pictures in the correct order.
Now tell the story in your own words.
How short can you make the story?

Puzzle 2

helpful   selfish

excited

fussy   glum

sad

Choose the words which best describe each character. Can you think of any more? Pretend to be one of the characters!

Answers

Puzzle 1

The correct order is:

1e, 2d, 3b, 4c, 5f, 6a

Puzzle 2

Mary: glum, sad

the fairy: excited, helpful